DR.TUSHAR DUBEY

OATH AND OBLIVION

The Warriors of Dharma

AF657992

BlueRose ONE.com
Stories Matter
NewDelhi • London

BLUEROSE PUBLISHERS
India | U.K.

Copyright © Dr.Tushar Dubey 2025

All rights reserved by author. No part of this publication may be reproduced, stored in a retrieval system or transmitted in any form or by any means, electronic, mechanical, photocopying, recording or otherwise, without the prior permission of the author. Although every precaution has been taken to verify the accuracy of the information contained herein, the publisher assume no responsibility for any errors or omissions. No liability is assumed for damages that may result from the use of information contained within.

BlueRose Publishers takes no responsibility for any damages, losses, or liabilities that may arise from the use or misuse of the information, products, or services provided in this publication.

BlueRose ONE
Stories Matter
NewDelhi • London

For permissions requests or inquiries regarding this publication, please contact:

BLUEROSE PUBLISHERS
www.BlueRoseONE.com
info@bluerosepublishers.com
+91 8882 898 898
+4407342408967

ISBN: 978-93-7139-359-1

Cover design: Daksh
Typesetting: Tanya Raj Upadhyay

First Edition: June 2025

Preface

Oath and Oblivion: The Warriors of Dharma is a poetic retelling of the Mahabharata through the inner worlds of its two most resolute yet tragic figures—Karna and Bhishma. This epic-in-verse explores the lives of the Sun-born and the oath-bound, men who chose loyalty over legacy and silence over survival. From Karna's divine birth and rejection, to Bhishma's vow of celibacy and moral dilemma, each poem unearths the burdens they bore for honor and duty. Their destinies unfold across flaming chariots, cursed vows, and aching silences as they confront dharma in its most complex form. Through lyrical stanzas and mythic imagery, the book becomes a meditation on sacrifice, righteousness, and the loneliness of those who stand by their word—no matter the cost. A timeless tribute to unsung valor, Oath and Oblivion is both a literary homage and a spiritual journey into the heart of epic heroism.

Table of Contents

PART 1- KAUNTEYA

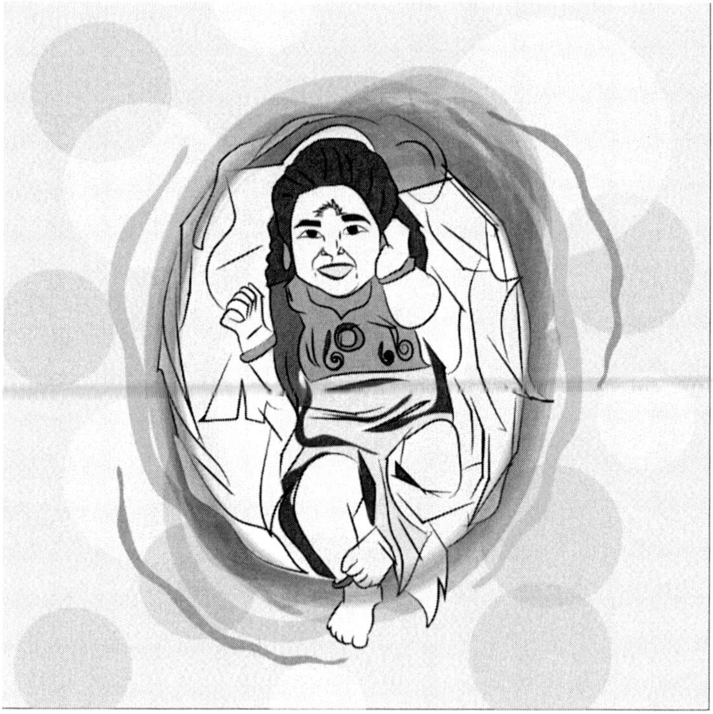

The Birth of Karna

O Mother Pritha, your summons won't be in vain,
My spark shall dwell in your womb, valiant and brave of brain.
No blemish shall mark your maidenly grace—
Yet truth remains: you'll bear the Sun's embrace.

The cosmic cycle reached its destined hour,
From Kunti's womb emerged the Sun God's power.
Four directions flared with solar might—
Yet why did Kunti not smile in that radiant light?

"What gaze will this world upon me cast?
Can a virgin mother from shame move past?"
Her mind was a storm, restless, unclear—
Though light held her child, her heart drowned in fear.

She stood at a fork, her fate to choose—
Motherly love or honor to lose.
She chose her name, let her heart grow cold—
O Pritha! A babe in arms, yet his tale left untold.

Unblessed was she—no milk to give,
No lullabies for the child to live.

With hardened will, she left him to fate,
In a bamboo basket, she sealed his state.

Thus fate began a different script—
To Radha's arms the infant slipped.
That barren heart bloomed into a stream,
As breastfed milk flowed in a mother's dream.

The Sun, moved by love so pure,
Blessed her heart forevermore.
From heaven's vaults a voice did ring:
"O blessed mother, your praises shall kings sing!"

"From this day forth, by your love he shall rise,
No longer Kaunteya, but Radheya in mortal eyes."

Karna's Education

No longer the Sun's child—now a charioteer's son,
Bound by caste, his path to knowledge was undone.
Though might surged through his elephantine arms,
He was denied the right to wield war's charms.

"O Guru Drona, accept me as your humble ward,
Shower me with wisdom, your knowledge be my reward."
But Drona's words struck sharp as spear or dart—
"Leave, O boy, your birth disqualifies your heart."

Yet Karna, the Sun's spark, would never flee,
A sage with an axe would soon his teacher be.
To learn the craft, he veiled his name and face,
And donned a Brahmin's form to earn his place.

Each word his teacher spoke, he obeyed with grace,
Even Parashurama saw no deceit in his face.
To have a student so devout, so true—
The warrior-saint felt blessed through and through.

The fire of Karna's wrath could scorch the skies,
He could turn mere straw into death's surprise.

With armor and earrings, his power grew vast,
Yet in time's shadow, no might would last.

One day, he cradled his master's head in rest,
A worm bit deep into Karna's thigh and nest.
Though blood streamed down in a crimson tide,
The warrior sat still, like a mountain wide.

When the sage awoke and saw the red flood,
Fury in his eyes blazed hot as his blood.
Karna bowed low, confessed his guise—
The truth poured forth, no hint of lies.

The sage's anger could split the sky,
He cursed him with a sorrowful sigh:
"When in your need, your moment is near,
You'll forget your skills—be gripped by fear."

Karna did not plead, nor cursed his fate,
He walked on calm, bearing time's heavy weight.

The Rise of the Prince of Anga

The day had come to showcase might,
Where kings displayed their valorous right.
The royal sons with pride did gleam,
While echoing cheers fed the king's esteem.

Each warrior stood with power grand—
One's arms could crush a thousand with a hand.
Another's mace sent foes to flight,
A third with arrows dazzled the sight.

Skill met skill with fierce parade,
But no one knew whose fame would fade.
Then Arjuna rose with bow in hand—
Applause resounded across the land.

Bheeshma watched in silent awe,
Drona's heart swelled with pride and law.
"You are supreme," said the sage with grace—
When a lion's roar tore through the place.

"O revered teacher, halt your claim,
Until I match him—let me earn my name!"
"Who dares disturb this sacred rite?"
"Name yourself, O challenger of Arjuna's might!"

"I pull no royal chariot, wear no crown,
But in my blood, true valor's found.
I am Karna—not a prince, but son of a charioteer,
Yet face me, Arjun, without fear!"

"You dare compare? You bear no throne—
This match is meant for kings alone!"
But cunning Shakuni whispered wise,
"To win this soul is Duryodhan's prize."

The eldest Kaurava, bold and grim,
Marked Karna's brow with blood from limb.
He crowned him lord of Anga's land—
A kingdom placed in Karna's hand.

No victor named, no loser shamed,
But Karna's name in glory flamed.
That day he earned both crown and fame—
From charioteer's son to Anga's name.

"O friend," he vowed, "your debt I'll bear,
Your shield I'll be, in life or snare.
This bond of ours shall never fade—
For Kuru's cause, my life is laid."

The Tale of Dishonor

Before the war, a tale unfolds—
Of royal halls and hearts gone cold.
Where queens were shamed and honor died,
And warriors sat with eyes cast wide.

The king of dharma, lost in dice,
Let fate slip through with foolish vice.
Entranced by Shakuni's cunning throws,
He gambled all—the highs and lows.

Gone was wealth, gone was pride,
The empire lost in a single slide.
He placed his crown beneath their feet,
And bowed his head in grim defeat.

But sly Shakuni grinned once more,
"Play again! Win back what's yours from yore!"
Drawn by illusion, Yudhishthir fell—
One by one, his brothers as well.

Each wager cast them down in shame,
The sons of Kunti lost their flame.
And then he staked the final prize—
Their queen, Panchali, with tearful eyes.

A gasp arose—a thunderous shock!
No law, no code could this unlock.
Duryodhan roared with vile command:
"Drag her forth with ruthless hand!"

And so, in court of kingly pride,
A woman's soul was crucified.
Hair dragged through stone, her cloth was torn—
The halls of justice now forlorn.

She clutched her robe, her honor tight,
Her cries of pain echoed through night.
But silence ruled those warrior men—
Their shame forever inked by pen.

Then Krishna heard her silent call,
From Dwaraka, he crossed it all.
He cloaked her form in endless thread,
And turned the tide from shame to dread.

No longer meek, her fire arose,
A fury that no wind could close.
"I swear," she cried, "by every star—
This insult shall spark a world at war!

O Kuru kings, if courage stays,
Then meet my wrath in coming days!"

Thus from the court her fire did rise—
And turned the dice to a war-scarred prize.

The game of chance, the shame so vast,
Lit the flame for Mahabharat's blast.

The Sorrow of Kurukshetra

Come, hear the tale I now must share,
Of blood-soaked lands and war's despair.
In my embrace the great war burned,
Where kin on kin in hatred turned.

On day one, Arjuna laid down his bow,
Gripped by fear, with head hung low.
Then Krishna spoke with truth and grace—
The Gita's flame lit time and space.

He rose anew with karma's creed,
And blew his conch to start the deed.
I turned from land of sacred lore,
To death's own field forevermore.

Ten days passed—my soils turned red,
A thousand heads lay cold and dead.
Then came a sight that stole my breath:
Arjun raised Bheeshma to his bed of death.

The thunder of weapons split the air,
And still no side could victory snare.
Then Drona wove the fatal snare—
A chakra-vyuha none could bear.

The thirteenth day, the sun did fade,
For Abhimanyu fell—betrayed.
On day fourteen, Krishna hid the light,
And Arjun swore to end the fight.

Then Drona rose like fire and flame,
But lies of loss sealed his name.
His fall came sharp with duty grim—
Love for his son became death for him.

Seventeen days of endless cries,
Then Karna roared with fiery eyes.
Fate gave the word, and so did I—
I held his wheel as he met the sky.

That sun-born soul, that generous hand,
Now lay as dust upon my land.
Even I, this sacred ground,
Was stained by fate where death was crowned.

Eighteenth dawn—what then remained?
Duryodhan, broken, lone and pained.
He called for war, a final fight,
But Bheem struck down his royal might.

I heard their war cries pierce the skies,
I've seen the widows' endless cries.

Not just Arjuna heard divine insight—
Even I was taught by Krishna's light.

The heroes who walked upon my face,
Found timeless glory in death's embrace.
I am Kurukshetra—field of war,
I cradle both wound and warrior.

Abhimanyu and the Spiral of Doom

He marched like time, a blazing fire,
The thirteenth day would rise much higher.
A deadly trap was now designed—
The chakra-vyuha, cruel and blind.

Drona roared like a lion proud,
While cries of pain rose through the crowd.
Ten directions rang with dread,
As Kurukshetra turned blood-red.

"How shall we breach this wicked snare?"
The Pandavs stood in blank despair.
"This wheel of death no one can break—
Save Arjun's might for dharma's sake."

But where was he, the archer prime?
They feared that now had come their time.
Until a voice, so fierce, so bold—
A youth stepped forth with fire untold.

"I'll go, O father, I'll storm the gate—
Their jeers and pride I'll devastate!"
No lullaby had blessed his ear,
Just tales of war from those held dear.

Perhaps fate chose this mighty frame—
To blaze within this deadly game.

With eyes aglow and heart aflame,
To battlefield the young lion came.
He tore the wheel, defied the dread—
The Kauravs feared, their glory fled.

His valor shocked the Kuru line,
His sword was swift, his aim divine.
Like lightning crashing through a storm,
He stood alone, a fearless form.

They struck him down with brutal blows,
Yet still he fought, unfazed by foes.
Their cowardice reached its wicked peak—
For never had war been fought so weak.

At last he fell, with pride intact—
A warrior by destiny exact.
Believe this truth: the stars conspired,
To script a saga through one so fired.

The Gift of Armor and Earrings

His body, like thunder, in blood now shone,
His valor unmatched, by all gods known.
Even Indra, with all his pride and might,
Stood speechless at Karna's fearless sight.

The lord of gods had changed his guise,
A beggar cloaked in humble lies.
But Karna saw beyond the veil,
And chose his dharma not to fail.

He carved from flesh his divine shield—
The armor that made no man yield.
He offered the gift without regret,
While crimson stains his chest beset.

The earth did tremble at his cry,
The heavens stirred, the gods drew nigh.
Even ghostly realms in awe did quake,
At such a gift, for dharma's sake.

The maidens of the sky were torn,
By love for him who bled and borne.
For Radheya stood, his soul alight,
His frame a blaze in the morning light.

"O Lord of Storms," he calmly said,
"Reveal thy form—no longer dread.
I know your heart as father knows son—
Now take your gift, my vow is done.

If pleased, then offer what I ask—
A weapon sure, to aid my task."

"Do not mistake my wounds for loss,
My arms still bear a hero's cross.
Though stripped of shield and earring's gold,
I burn with wrath both fierce and bold.

Hear me, O Indra, mark this vow—
No force shall stop my chariot now.
The battlefield shall know my name,
And shudder 'neath my arrows' flame.

My quiver shall write my song in red,
With blood, the tale of Karna spread.
Upon this field, I'll stand alone—
And make the gods themselves atone."

Karna's State of Mind

I know the path I choose is dark,
Yet still I bear this fateful mark.
Though wrong may trail the steps I tread,
I'll raise Kaurava's flag till I fall dead.

I'll keep my vow, though hands may shake,
And strike my brothers for dharma's sake.
Yes, even against the Lord I'll stand—
For fate demands this in its hand.

In Kurukshetra I shall rise,
A fire beneath the stormy skies.
My bow shall blaze like Yama's rod—
My wrath shall stain the land of God.

Let Arjuna come—my bolts will fly,
His chariot shall kiss the sky.
Let widows wail and mothers cry—
Today the sons of Kunti die.

The heavens will rain a storm of flame,
This maddened beast will not be tamed.
If Indra comes to block my way,
Even he shall taste dismay.

I know full well my end is near,
I know my fate—I show no fear.
Till breath departs, my arms shall sway—
Then death shall crown me in its way.

With bow in hand, my soul shall burn—
And in my death, I shall return.
When battle ends and silence reigns,
Call me not fallen—but one who remains.

When Karna Brings the Storm

String your bow firm, O Parth, he comes to fight—
The Sun-born blaze shall scorch with light.
Though stripped of shield and golden mail,
His burning gaze will make you pale.

Peer once into those eyes aglow,
Before your first strike, and you'll know—
A volcano's wrath, a doomsday tide,
In Karna's soul and stance abide.

Beware, O warrior, tread with care—
Today he'll show the art of war laid bare.
With arms like gods, he'll raise his bow,
And shake the worlds with every blow.

When Karna roars in battle's call,
Three realms shall tremble, kingdoms fall.
His wheels may quake, the Earth may rend,
As time itself nears fateful end.

His bowstring forms death's noose today,
For this one hour he's longed to slay.
O mighty soul, prepare your breath—
Your valor now shall face its test.

Yes, your charioteer may rule all fate,
And Hanuman on your banner wait—
But pride must fall, you must amend,
For even bare, Karna's might won't bend.

Divine weapons shall fiercely clash,
And signal an age's final flash.
So many heroes fate shall claim,
And twilight mask the sun in flame.

Yet truth be told—today, even Krishna sighs,
For he too knows a hero dies.
The Earth shall lose a titan's grace,
As Heaven prepares to light its face.

So, Parth, prepare—be still, be brave,
For now the lion of war shall rave.
Tie your string strong, for in the fray,
Karna shall bring the world doomsday.

Kaunteya Versus Kaunteya

Time etched its tale on destiny's scroll,
Kurukshetra roared—fate took its toll.
Among the echoes of battle and flame,
One Kaunteya stood to face the same.

On one side, Gandiva's string did sing,
On the other, eyes like the morning's wing.
No matter who wins, the earth shall cry—
For today, a mother shall bid one son goodbye.

Krishna had foreseen this sorrowed day,
When brother from brother would turn away.
Though Kali's age was far in line,
Today it came before its time.

One mother begged beneath the sun,
"I bore not five—but truly one more son."
She told the Sun-born of her plea,
To spare her sons, but he broke silently.

The queen's last hope was turned to shame,
As Karna chose honor over name.
Now armed with truth and veiled in pain,
A brother would draw his blood in vain.

Win or fall—this day will stay,
In memory's heart till time decays.
The one who strikes shall claim the tale,
The one who falls shall wear death's veil.

A Kaunteya must his fate embrace,
One shall never see his mother's face.
One shall rise with dharma's hand—
The other fall, yet proudly stand.

Karna: The Thunder Without Armor

Though stripped of armor, I still remain—
A wrathful storm, a god of pain.
As long as Victory's bow I wield,
My blazing might shall not be sealed.

My soul will not from body part,
Till I unleash the fire in my heart.
See these arrows in my sheath—
They'll rain down ruin and summon death.

Who dares stand before my chariot's way,
Shall take the path where Yama sways.
Let the world now cry and quake—
When Radheya's bowstring starts to shake.

I am no mere soldier of clay—
I'm brother to Bheeshma, in arms and way.
The earth shall shudder at my word,
When vows I make and wrath is stirred.

What art of war can I not command?
Even Brahmastra heeds my hand.
At my call it breaks its chain—
No force resists my fiery reign.

The soil of war shall drink deep red,
As Chandi dances on the dead.
A tale of slaughter I shall write—
With arrows forged from blazing light.

Mark my words—the world shall see,
What Karna's fierce might truly be.
When madness grips this tusked wild beast,
The gods themselves shall fear the feast.

Even Parth's charioteer shall shake,
When Radheya makes the heavens quake.
And cosmos wide will sing my praise,
When I send Arjuna's chariot ablaze.

I know my fate—I shall fall brave,
But Duryodhan, your life I gave.
Before I leave, let all behold—
A friendship sung in stories bold.

With pride my saga shall be sung,
Across all time and every tongue.
For even in death, the world shall say:
"This Karna was deathless—Mṛityunjaya."

The Dialogue of Karna's Bow

"O Radheya, do not cast me aside!
The battle still roars, fate must be defied.
Though your armor and crown are gone,
Your soul remains like thunder drawn.

I swear upon my string and steel—
With every twang, the heavens will reel.
Who needs arrows to strike the foe?
Let my roar split hearts below!"

"Why did you promise, O noble one,
To the mother who hid her only son?
What kind of mother casts her child adrift,
Yet seeks his mercy as a gift?"

"Forget, for a moment, that you are the kind,
Whose hands once gave and heart was blind.
Feel my weight—I know your fire,
Your arms still burn with battle's desire."

"These broken wheels won't hold you still—
Summon the Sun with blazing will!
String me now, let fate be braved—
Let destiny itself be enslaved."

"O warrior of war, arise once more—
Your vow awaits, the gods implore!
Become death's shadow with my string—
Let Parth now face the reckoning."

"Behold! He lifts Gandiva's bow,
Let not your heart be weak and low.
Forget he is your brother true—
In war, no ties must follow through."

"I am not shattered—I still remain!
Let not your silence make hope vain.
I do not lie like falsehood's king—
Your victory lies in how you string."

But as the bow still whispered brave,
Arjuna loosed the bolt he gave.
It struck the unarmed, stripped of fight—
And honor bled into the night.

"O Radheya! Radheya!" the silence cried,
As the mighty gave, though wrongly died.
"Why did you leave me in this pain?
With me in hand, none could you slain!"

You fell through trickery, fate's cruel song—
But in death, O Karna, you proved fate wrong.

The Grief of Karna's Chariot Wheel

O fate! Today, to you I bow—
I halted in battle, and broke my vow.
A wheel I was for a warrior grand,
Yet now I sink into this sacred land.

Upon my axis, Radheya rose,
A flame so fierce, he scorched his foes.
Even Madhava's heart did shake—
For Karna stood, a storm awake.

With power, he split the sky apart,
No trick could match his dauntless heart.
Both gods and mortals feared his tread—
Had Krishna not deceived, Arjun lay dead.

He bore his strength with godlike pride,
And shook the world from every side.
Even Shyam, the trickster's mind,
Knew Karna's fire no fate could bind.

His gaze erupted like a star,
His bow could bend the world from far.
Warriors flinched beneath his name,
And victory dared not claim his flame.

To carry him, I was proud and blessed—
Yet fate ordained a crueler test.
O Radheya, now you must fall,
Leave behind this bloodstained hall.

Abandon this chariot—ascend in light,
Don celestial robes and end the fight.
Look! The Sun himself now comes to take,
His son from war, from pain, from ache.

See how the golden chariot nears—
A father calls beyond the spheres.
The Sun sets not in grief today,
But hides his tears in twilight gray.

I am no longer wheel of war—
Now time's own turning I endure.
But know this well, O peerless one—
Your tale, your flame, shall never be undone.

And saying so, the wheel gave way,
And Karna too passed from the day.
His bonds were loosed, his soul took flight—
A hero crowned in heaven's light.

Krishna's Battle Cry

"O Parth, delay no longer now,
String your bow, fulfill your vow!
Aim your arrow, strike with flame—
Let Radheya fall to dharma's name."

"Leave right and wrong to me, O friend,
This war must meet its destined end.
Turn your aim where justice calls,
For silence now is where duty falls."

"This chance shall not again arise,
If Karna lifts his bow, he shall not die.
Defeat him now before he stands,
Or none can stop his wrathful hands."

"Did he not call Panchali foul?
Did he not join in evil's prowl?
You call him weaponless—forget not,
It was he who left Abhimanyu to rot."

"As long as Radheya breathes in might,
The Pandavs cannot win this fight.
He stands between your crown and fate—
Break him now before too late!"

"He is no brother now you see,
But shield of Kauravas' tyranny.
Strike him now—this moment weighs,
More than a thousand yesterdays."

"Have faith in me—his time is near,
He'll meet his end with honor clear.
His name shall live in every tale,
As one who stood, though doomed to fail."

"His guru's curse comes forth today,
He forgets the arts that once held sway.
His memory fails, his skill is lost—
Now strike, O Parth, whatever the cost!"

"Don't look into his eyes so deep—
Their silent fire may make you weep.
Their pain may shake your soul apart,
But now you must strike with steel, not heart."

"Free him from this cursed life,
End his burden, end his strife.
He has suffered long, too long this flame—
Let now the Lord reclaim his name."

"Strike your arrow, raise your cry—
Today the Mahabharat shall fly!
Yes, you'll win—but mark this day:
Radheya shall be remembered as Death's delay."

The Lament of Arjun's Arrow

I cannot answer your call today,
Forgive me, Parth—I must not slay.
Let me not strike that noble frame,
Let me not bear this cursed name.

You bid me fly at Krishna's cry,
But I am torn—I can't comply.
To slay a man who stands unarmed,
Is this the code that dharma charmed?

Bound I am to duty's path,
To strike the foe and wield your wrath.
But look, O Parth—he stands alone,
His wheel is sunk, his might overthrown.

Know this, O son of Pandu's line—
When loosed from you, I reigned divine.
Your every battle I helped win,
But now I shake from deep within.

For there he stands—a blazing sun,
And I must end what he's begun.
How can I strike that radiant face,
Born of Surya's mighty grace?

So be it, O bannered king,
I'll carry out your reckoning.
Let glory shield your honored name,
And I shall bear eternal shame.

But hear this vow as I take flight—
Though I may strike and dim his light,
No blade can claim his soul so high—
Though you may win, **he** shall not die.

He falls today, but not in vain—
The heavens rise to call his name.
O Arjun, you win this sacred war,
But Karna shines on, a deathless star.

The Fire Ordeal of Death

She knew the hour had now begun,
To test her fire against the Sun.
Trembling still, yet bound by fate,
She neared the hero Heaven would await.

Before her stood the blazing soul—
A warrior fierce, sublime and whole.
His eyes burned bright, his body scarred,
His breath was calm, his gaze unmarred.

"O Lord of Yog," she cried in dread,
"Grant me strength to strike him dead.
Let not his flame consume my will,
Let not this task my spirit kill.

If you promise me his soul tonight,
Then I shall walk into this fight.
But tell me, which chain or mighty blow,
Can pierce that chest where gods bestow?

This is no mortal I must face—
But one who walks with Titan grace.
He is no man to meekly fall,
His wrath shall thunder through us all!"

She wept beneath her darkened veil,
Yet Radheya saw her grief and pale.
He smiled and raised a hand to bless—
"Come forth, O Death, I acquiesce."

"O highest truth, unbind me now—
To thee alone I make this vow.
You are beyond, you are my gate—
Now take me through the hands of fate."

And saying so, the lion lay,
His crown cast down, his breath gave way.
She kissed his brow and pulled him free,
From pain, from war, from destiny.

The Sun-born gave his final gift—
His life, that worlds might one day lift.
The hero climbed his final cart—
To journey back from whence he'd start.

Now crowned by flames, by stars, by grace—
Mṛityunjay rose to the Sun's embrace.

Karna's Final Words

Here, O Mother, my duty's done—
I've kept my vow, my life is gone.
I gave my breath as alms today,
My promise now is swept away.

But why the tears upon my face?
You cast me off in time's embrace.
You left me crying, lost, alone—
Why mourn the seed you'd never sown?

You weep now for the child you spurned—
The same whose cries you never heard.
Look now—your five sons live in pride,
Then let me go, no guilt to hide.

You came too late, with selfish plea,
I read your love's hypocrisy.
Before you leave, just tell me this—
Why was my birth your cursed abyss?

Why bring me forth to leave behind,
Condemned by fate, ignored by kind?
I bore a gift no one could match—
Yet I was locked without a latch.

Born of the Sun, with golden skin,
I too had claims to live within
Your arms, your song, your name, your light—
Why make me hide my truest right?

I cried in hunger, lost in cold,
But never once your arms would hold.
When caste and shame rained down on me,
You never stood to set me free.

When mocked for birth, when scorned for name,
You chose your silence, cloaked in shame.
When Indra came to steal my pride,
You stood afar and never cried.

You never came—I wept in vain.
You never came—I bore the pain.
You never came, while time betrayed—
And with each day, my trust decayed.

So why now come, to mourn and weep,
While I prepare for final sleep?
Look there! My father comes in gold—
The Sun descends, his arms unfold.

Mark this, O Queen, and hear my will—
You may forget me, but I still

Shall rise with pride in heaven's flame,
Yet never again bear your name.

I'll shine as Radheya, ever free—
But never again as Kaunteya be.

The Blaze of Karna's Pyre

Even the Ashwamedha seemed pale that day,
Before the fire where Karna lay.
The son of the Sun, wrapped in flame,
Ascended beyond all earthly fame.

The five Kaunteyas stood in grief—
Warriors silenced by disbelief.
Heroes don't weep, the wise have said—
Yet tears welled up for the fallen dead.

They struck their kin, their elder slain,
And bore the weight of brother's pain.
No victor now, no crown of light—
For dharma dimmed in Karna's sight.

The Earth stood still in shadowed gloom,
While heaven's halls rejoiced in bloom.
Gandharvas danced, the apsaras sang,
The sky itself in praises rang.

Yakshas trimmed the stars with gold,
To welcome him, the just and bold.
Today the gates of heaven swung—
For a warrior true, a soul unsung.

The Sun beamed proud through tearful rays,
As flames consumed his child in blaze.
Even Surya's chariot, bright and wide,
Seemed dim beside his son's last ride.

From his pyre rose a light so pure,
It lit the stars and skies obscure.
The universe, in awe, stood hushed—
As light and heat from him now rushed.

The gods themselves left thrones above,
To bow before his soul with love.
They hailed his name in sacred hymn—
For none could match the fire in him.

His life became a lesson vast—
Of valor, truth, and trials passed.
The flames then claimed what Earth once bore—
And merged him with the Sun once more.

He rose, the Mṛityunjay divine,
On chariot made of golden shine.
And in that blaze, the world could see—
That Karna lives eternally.

The Sorrow of the Sun

Bound to duty, I must ride—
Even as my son lay crucified.
His light now dimmed upon the land,
While I still moved by fate's command.

O how I longed to pause, descend—
To hold his head, my child, my friend.
To kiss his brow and take his pain,
But duty chained my golden reign.

I watched him fall—I saw him bleed,
My heart burned fierce, yet none could heed.
The Sun, so bright, shed silent flame,
And wept unseen, consumed by shame.

They tricked him, broke him, scarred his truth—
My radiant son, robbed in his youth.
Yet bound I was, by time and law,
To watch in silence what I saw.

Yes, I am the axis of the skies—
But what is light when justice dies?
For even I, the cosmic king,
Could not protect my sunlit wing.

When born, he flowed on rivers still—
A mother's fear, a heartless will.
They called him low, denied his worth,
Though gods themselves had carved his birth.

His teacher cursed, his peers betrayed—
While kings and queens his worth outweighed.
And I, who knew his soul was flame,
Still bore the silence, cloaked in shame.

But now, at last, his war is done,
No more shall Karna fight or run.
He's battled fate and faced the storm—
And left this world in hero's form.

Now rise, my child, ascend with grace,
And light the stars with your embrace.
Ride this chariot of golden rays—
Let Earth remember all your days.

Your name shall blaze in every age,
Beyond all wrong, beyond all rage.
For though I ride and never rest—
Your glory shines within my chest.

The Lament of Karna's Wife

Why do you boast, O Panchali, in red attire so proud?
My empty parting, my shattered vow, cries louder
than your shroud.
You paint your forehead in victory's hue—
But it's my widowhood that colors you.

No valor won this bloody game,
No dharma carved your golden name.
This war, this throne, this hollow prize—
Was fed by schemes and whispered lies.

You call yourself queen of righteous flame,
Yet my tears curse that stolen claim.
O Pandavas, what glory is this?
You slew your kin in war's abyss.

Your Krishna, too, who speaks of grace,
Took Karna's blood to light your place.
No tilak brightens your noble brow—
That red is his—it bleeds there now.

You plead no guilt, say none were vile,
And justify your means in style.

But weigh his valor 'gainst your schemes—
And kingdoms crack at Radheya's screams.

They spoke of law, of noble thread,
Yet cursed and mocked the life he led.
They feared his rise, his might, his name—
So cloaked their war in dharma's frame.

O Draupadi, no queen are you—
This crown was begged, not earned through true.
Look at the rod that claims the throne—
It rose from ashes not your own.

My widowhood shall curse this age,
And write the end of every page.
Let Kali rise, let justice fall—
For dharma died in Karna's call.

You'll sit in courts with jeweled grace—
While I burn with none to embrace.
But know this well: while you reign high,
I ride with him, where gods still cry.

For on his pyre I too shall lay—
And ride with him the solar way.
While you wear crowns and sip your wine,
I'll soar with stars—forever divine.

The Breaking of Arjun's Pride

You are no hero of this grand tale—
You were lifted high so you wouldn't fail.
This throne you boast, you did not earn—
It was gifted by fate at every turn.

You weren't the one to build this height—
You were carried up through borrowed might.
This crown you wear with swelling chest—
Was paid in blood by one oppressed.

Your song was written by another hand—
A tale composed you barely planned.
Think not you're flawless, bold, divine—
Your faults were veiled by fate's design.

You're not the ocean, boundless, vast—
You're but a well—fed from the past.
You weren't the doer, nor the end—
Just one more pawn fate chose to send.

Remember this…

Karna did not fall—he was made to bow.

And you did not win—they raised you somehow.

PART 2
GANGEYA

The Birth of Bhishma

(*Original: "Bhishma ka Janm"*)

Have you heard of Devavrata, the vow-bound flame,
Whose iron resolve earned the "Bhishma" name?
His word, once spoken, never bent or strayed,
A warrior eternal, whose legacy never decayed.

The mighty king Shantanu ruled with might,
Across the earth, his valor shone bright.
Nymphs would bend to serve his throne,
Yet his heart beat for Ganga alone.

He wooed her with grace, and she did agree,
But laid down a vow with no room for plea—
"Let our children be mine to claim,
And their fate be bound to my name."

Seven sons she bore, then gave to the stream,
A sight too cruel to remain a dream.
Shantanu wept, unable to bear,
The eighth child spared by his despair.

"O Goddess!" he cried, "Why such a deed?"
"Why drown our sons, my soul you bleed!"

She answered with sorrow and mystic tone,
"These children are divine, not your own.

They were cursed in realms beyond your view,
Freed from the cycle by waters true.
But this last one, Devavrata bold,
Shall live on earth with courage untold."

Thus was born the one divine,
Who'd guard his oath through endless time.
From heaven's grace to earthly flame,
The world would tremble at Bhishma's name.

The Turmoil Within Bhishma

The dreadful vow he once had sworn,
With steadfast will, he daily bore.
Time's wheel turned slow but sure,
And aged Satyavati grew insecure.

With heart entrapped in motherly chains,
She placed weak Vichitravirya on throne's reins.
Knowing well his strength was small,
Yet forced the decision, against royal call.

"O Bhishma!" she cried, "now it's your hour—
To find him brides with valor and power.
Ride to Kashi, with arms of might,
Bring daughters for your brother's right."

Bound by honor to throne and state,
Gangeya set forth to meet his fate.
At swayamvar, with strength he shone,
And seized the princesses, not one—three alone.

But Amba spoke her heart's desire,
For Shalwa's love still burned like fire.
This plea would spark a tragic tide,
A tale of curses, death, and pride.

Bhishma's Last Stand

Bhishma fought like Time itself unfurled,
Thirteen days passed in a war-torn world.
Like death incarnate he struck his foes—
The field of Kurukshetra darkly glows.

He vowed destruction of Pandava might,
Even Krishna frowned at Arjun's plight.
No man could halt Ganga's fiery tide—
His arrows rained like fate defied.

Whole armies fell beneath his storm,
As Bhishma's wrath took lethal form.
He challenged Arjun with roaring flame,
His voice like thunder, calling his name.

He who once rocked the child to sleep,
Now loosed his shafts in volleys deep.
The hands that once had crowned his kin
Now hurled sharp death from deep within.

The clang of Gandiva rent the sky,
The Vayavya's whistle pierced on high.
Even Time's tongue, unseen but near,
Lapped hungrily toward each fearless peer.

Two titans clashed with every skill—
The field grew still, as blood would spill.
Bhishma, the grandsire, proud and great—
Now faced the hour decreed by fate.

The Mirror Within: A Dialogue Between Karna and Bhishma

Bhishma:

O Radheya! Within your soul,
I glimpse my own—a mirrored whole.
Dear brother-in-arms, your fate and mine
Are bound by threads both sharp and fine.

Like me, by mother's hands denied,
Love from her arms you too were deprived.
No nectar of her breast I knew,
You too were cast to fate's dark hue.

As a child, I cried out "Mother, where?"
Tell me—did someone hold you there?
Yet I envy that Radha's grace
Gave your sorrow a gentler place.

I was bartered for Satyavati's gain,
A pawn in fate's imperial game.
You too were steadfast to your word,
In loyalty's flame, your spirit stirred.

I stood as shield for Hastinapur's reign,
You fought for Duryodhan through every strain.

I served the throne and its decree,

You never failed your friend's plea.

Your loyalty burned like sacred fire,

Your truth stood firm through flood and pyre.

Our vows, though different, both were pure—

Dharma's weight, we both endure.

Bhishma's Final Question

Who shall bind these mountain arms with thread?
What curse shall pierce this iron chest of dread?
This isn't a warrior whose might shall fade—
Nor is Karna a man who'll be easily betrayed.

Before me now, stands fate so grim,
I am darkness, he's the solar brim.
I tremble now, my end seems near,
Will Time dissolve before his searing glare?

Yet Karna smiles—undaunted, still—
His calm assurance bends death to will.
He grants me safety, spares his dart,
While death, now humbled, draws near to start.

"O Eternal Truth," he softly prays,
"Unbind my bonds, end my worldly days.
O Death, you are fearless, embrace me now,"
With those brave words, he took a vow.

The lion-hearted laid his head to rest,
Death kissed his brow and freed his chest.
The Son of the Sun gave life as a gift,
On chariot of light, he made his final lift.